The Old

Red Truck

Lisa Miller

For the Dad in the red truck--

You are worth the waiting and searching.

Tick tock, 5 o'clock!
The old red truck will soon come down the block.

"Mama, Mama, will you carry me please?
I like to ride up high where I can see."

Over her shoulder I point to the sky
and wave to the helicopter flying by.

The pilot waves back, happy as can be
but he's not the one I really want to see.

Off in the distance a motorcycle hums,
     and I begin to wonder, will the truck ever come?

Up at the intersection, brakes gently squeak,
"Is that him?" I wonder, "Is it the red truck I seek?"

But around the corner the mailman turns
and so my heart still longs and yearns.

Then all of the sudden Mama points and shouts!
"I see it, I see it! The red truck is in route!"

The old red truck becomes larger as it drives near,
and all of the sudden I see the driver quite clear!

Dad swings open the door and I jump inside,
me on his lap and Mama outside.

Hands on the steering wheel and eyes on the road,
I get to help drive the last 30 yards home.

We'll wait 12 hours

We'll wait 7 months

We'll wait forever
for our love.